Things That Go

Written by Erin Rose Grobarek
Illustrated by Paul Dronsfield and Maryn Arreguín

Published by Sequoia Children's Publishing,
an imprint of Phoenix International Publications, Inc.

8501 West Higgins Road, Suite 790
Chicago, Illinois 60631

59 Gloucester Place
London W1U 8JJ

www.sequoiakidsbooks.com

10 9 8 7 6 5 4 3 2 1

ISBN 978-1-64269-043-9

The roads in the country bend and wind. How many vehicles can you find?

Digging, pulling,
and lifting up high,
Look for these machines
as they drive by:

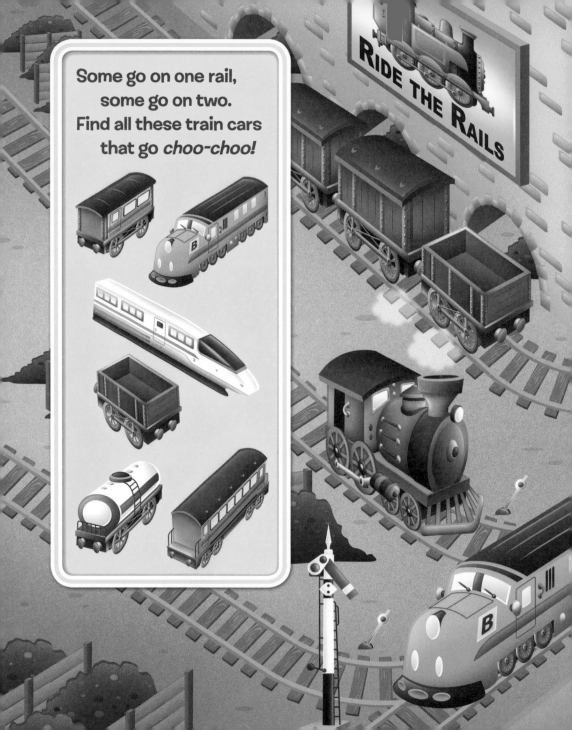

Some go on one rail,
some go on two.
Find all these train cars
that go *choo-choo!*

RIDE THE RAILS

Floating on waves,
or bobbing below,
Spot all these ships
that go with the flow:

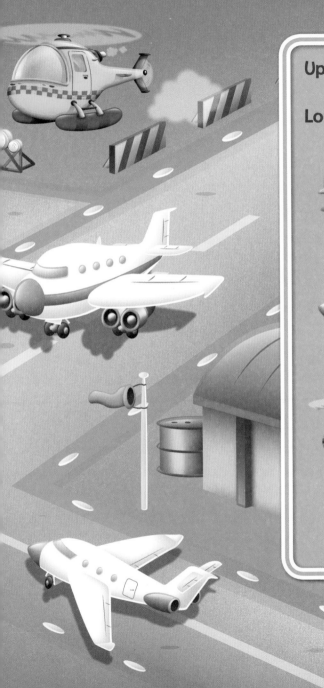

Up off the ground
and into the air,
Look for these things
that fly by with care:

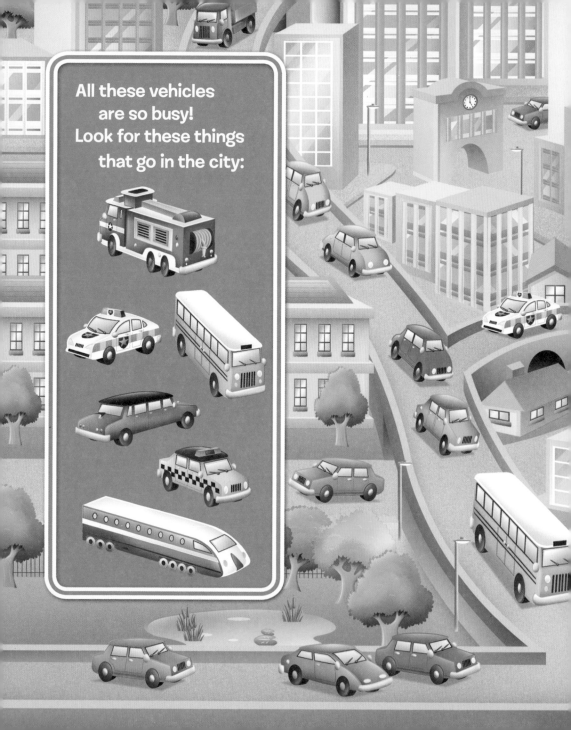

All these vehicles
are so busy!
Look for these things
that go in the city:

It's the end of the map,
but you can find more:

Then use this telescope
and explore!

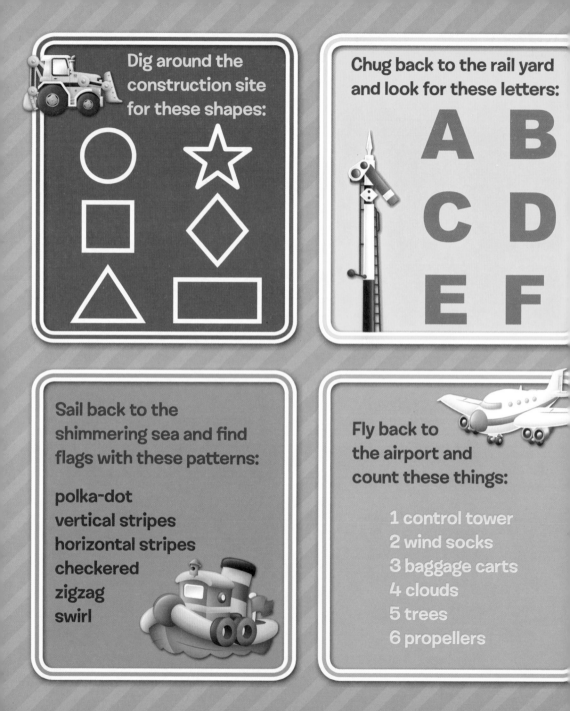

Dig around the construction site for these shapes:

Chug back to the rail yard and look for these letters:

A B
C D
E F

Sail back to the shimmering sea and find flags with these patterns:

polka-dot
vertical stripes
horizontal stripes
checkered
zigzag
swirl

Fly back to the airport and count these things:

1 control tower
2 wind socks
3 baggage carts
4 clouds
5 trees
6 propellers